Lani Loewen

MAUI MAUI

Written By:
STEPHEN COSGROVE

Illustrated By:
ROBIN JAMES

GROLIER ENTERPRISES INC.
Danbury, Connecticut

A Serendipity Book

Dedicated to the Lahaina Restoration
Society and their exceptional marine
program: WHALE WATCHERS.
Jim Luckey and his dedicated staff taught
me the true value of Maui-Maui and all
the other magnificent whales of the world.

Steve Cosgrove

To learn how you can help with
conserving and saving the wonderful
world of the whales, write to:
WHALE WATCHERS
C/O Lahaina Restoration Society
Lahaina-Maui, Hawaii

Seagulls soared like butterflies over the clear blue waters of the Pacific Ocean. Their wings dipped and tipped the waves as the wind gently floated them to some unknown destination.

Suddenly, the stillness of the ocean was broken by the mighty leap of a whale as it breached high into the air and crashed back into the sea. Soon the water was awash as an entire pod of whales flipped and frolicked in the crystal morning sunshine.

They floated and rolled in the sea, spouting water high into the air, and basked in the sunshine shower of rainbows they had created. The warm air nearly lulled the whales to sleep as they drifted gently in the blue Pacific waters.

Far off on the horizon a dozen or so strange little boats suddenly appeared, and the quiet solitude of the whales was broken by the loud, squeaky voices of small, furry creatures called Amomonies, who manned the sails.

The whales, with an unspoken signal, slid beneath the sea and quickly swam away.

The Amomonies, with much arm-waving, screaming and yelling, threw their nets into the water and began the daily chore of fishing.

As soon as the nets were filled with fish, the Amomonies pulled them aboard, dumping the fish into the bottom of the boat and tossing the nets back into the water. Their nets caught everything and anything: little fish, big fish, tuna, cod, and even an occasional octopus that happened, unfortunately, to be swimming by. The Amomonies really didn't care. They just threw them in the bottom of the boat, tossed the nets back into the water and fished some more.

They were always in such a hurry to catch a bunch of fish that one, or sometimes two, of the Amomonies would slip on a fish and fall into the water, catching himself in the net. It didn't matter to the other creatures; they would just haul in the nets and dump their soggy friend into the bottom of the boat with all the fish. Poor Amomony! He'd shake the water out of his fur, brush off the seaweed, climb back up on the deck of the ship and fish some more.

They fished like this for hours and hours. Waving their arms, screaming, and yelling, the Amomonies threw the nets in the water, filled them with fish, hauled in the nets, dumped the fish in the bottom of the boat and then started all over again.

Finally when their boats couldn't hold another fish without sinking, they set their sails and headed back to Amomony Island.

When they arrived back at their island, the other Amomonies helped them drag their boats onto the beach and unload all the fish they had caught. There were so many fish, baskets and baskets of them, that nobody even cared when a little stray kitten snitched one and hightailed it to the other side of the island.

When all the fish were cleaned, the queen of all the Amomonies, Mom Amomony, would cook the most delicious dishes you could ever imagine. She would cook fish stew, fried fish, fricasseed fish, roast fish, fish soup, and best of all, for dessert, fish pudding with seasoned seaweed sauce. Mom Amomony, just like the other Amomonies who always caught more fish than they could use, always cooked more fish than they could eat. "It didn't matter," they thought. "There's always more fish in the sea."

Once again, that very next morning, the Amomonies loaded their boats and set sail for the fishing grounds.

When they arrived, they began yelling, screaming, and waving their arms as they threw their nets into the sea. But before they had a chance to pull in the first net of fish, a large, magnificent whale breached and leaped high into the air crashing down on the Amomonies' nets.

Try as they might, the Amomonies could not haul in their nets with that monstrous whale holding on to the other end. They tugged and pulled to no avail. Finally out of frustration they cut the nets free and watched them sink to the bottom of the ocean.

The Amomonies sat around on their gently rocking boats trying to figure out what to do.

They thought and they thought and then one of the creatures said brightly, "I know! We've all got our old fishing poles aboard. If we can't net the fish we can catch them with hook, line, and sinker."

"Hmmm!" thought the other Amomonies. "It may take a little longer but we can still fill our boats with fish."

So they hurriedly gathered all the poles together, tied the hooks onto the lines, and cast them into the water. Just as one of the little creatures was about to hook the first fish, that very same whale came slipping up and out of the water, snatching the pole right out of his hands!

"This will never do!" they cried as they threw their poles down in disgust. "We must go back to the island and ask the queen what to do." With that they hurriedly set sail for home.

Well, as was usual when the boats returned, the other Amomonies rushed out to help unload all the fish that had been caught, but much to their dismay there wasn't a single fish to unload.

"What's the meaning of this!" shouted the queen of all the Amomonies, Mom Amomony.

The fishermen all knelt at her feet and cried, "We tried, oh great queen, but whenever we tried to catch any fish a mighty grey whale would steal our nets and our fishing poles. We didn't know what we should do."

"Poppycock!!" grumbled the queen. "First thing in the morning I will sail out and talk to this mighty whale of yours and I'll command him to leave you alone." With that she stomped back to her hut to prepare for the journey.

Bright and early the next morning the queen of all the Amomonies set out to find the great whale. She sailed all morning and long into the day but nowhere could she find the grey whale.

"Those lazy fishermen probably made up the whole thing. There isn't any whale at all!" Then, just to prove her point, she decided to fish for a little while. With much yelling, screaming, and waving of her arms she threw her net over the side of the boat. No sooner had the net touched the water than the great grey whale leaped high into the air and landed on top of the net.

"Now see here!" she shouted haughtily. "Why are you doing that? Give me back my net; I am causing you no harm!"

"Oh, but you are," said the whale. "My name is Maui-Maui and I am the leader of a small pod of whales who live peacefully in these waters. We didn't mind when you moved to the island and began to fish the sea. But now, because of your wastefulness there aren't enough fish for my fellow whales and we are going hungry."

"Oh, pooh!" grumbled Mom Amomony. "There's always been plenty of fish in the sea. I'll tell you what, Master Maui-Maui. I will swim with you and you may show me." With that she removed her sea shell cape and her palm leaf crown and leaped bravely into the water with the great grey whale.

"As you wish," said Maui-Maui quietly. "But I swim much faster than you. Hold on to my dorsal fin and I will show you an empty sea."

The queen did as he asked and they slowly sank into the deep blue water. Deeper and deeper they went and all the while they saw not one fish, not even a single solitary octopus.

Down and down they went and still not one fish was seen. Finally after searching every nook and cranny at the bottom of the sea they surfaced near the queen's boat and Maui-Maui carefully helped her onto the deck.

"I don't understand," she said, as she combed the seaweed from her hair. "There used to be so many fish. Where have they all gone?"

Maui-Maui thought for a moment and then carefully said, "You always caught more fish than you needed and you always cooked more fish than you needed. Now because of your wastefulness there aren't any fish at all."

"What are we to do?" she cried. "Without the fish we will surely starve."

"Come," said the great whale, "let me tow you back to your island and I will teach you and your people how to share your life with the sea." He carefully slipped the net over his head and quickly pulled the small boat back to the island.

When they got back to the island the other Amomonies were really scared to see such a large whale but the queen soon set them at ease and Maui-Maui began teaching them about conservation in the sea.

He taught them to catch only the full-grown fish and to throw the little ones back into the water so that they would have a chance to grow. He taught them the difference between the fishes and how to catch certain fish at certain times. He taught them to fish for only what they needed and to gently put the occasional octopus back in the water when it got caught in the nets. But most of all he taught them to love and respect the sea the way a farmer loves his land and cares for his animals.

From that day forward the Amomonies and the whales worked together hand in fin to make the ocean a finer place to live in.

The only time they ever had any trouble was when they would sight on the horizon a dozen or so strange little boats sailed by smooth-skinned creatures called Men.

SO, WHEN YOU ARE OUT FISHING
IN THE OCEANS, LAKES OR SEAS
REMEMBER MAUI-MAUI
AND THE LESSON OF THE AMOMONIES